BARRACUDA

· · · · **·** · · ·

THE FATE DIAMOND SERIES
BOOK 3

MAURY K. DOWNS
AND LORNA DOWNS

Barracuda

Copyright © 2024, Maury K. Downs and Lorna Downs
All rights reserved.
ISBN: 978-1-7351204-7-8

Published in the United States of America
By Jewel Sky Publications and Productions

Dedicated to

MKD, my husband, my captain and my soulmate. Through the years, I still feel the same tingly excitement that I felt when we first met. I love you so much.
My mother, children and grandchildren, you make my world a better place. I dearly love you all.
My Tabernero and Acob family, I didn't choose you, and nor did you choose me. You are God's gift to me and I am blessed to have you all be part of me. I love you all, kapamilya.
—LD

Mom, Dad, Ritha, Marcia, Michael, Ryan Kristoffer, Jasmin, Kristina, Gillian and our dear grandchildren.
And my dearest co-author and wife, Lorna.
You are all part of me.
—MKD

ABOUT THE AUTHOR

Maury K. Downs was born and raised in Los Angeles, California. He has had a rewarding previous career working as a health care provider. His joy is all things aviation, and he is a certificated pilot and flight instructor. He has traveled the world as an airline transport pilot. He holds a type rating in the "Queen of the skies" Boeing 747 and the Airbus 320. When he was a child, he enjoyed telling imaginary stories to his friends and family for their entertainment. He enjoys hearing the humorous cavorts and bold adventures of people's travels. "The Way You See Me Now" was his debut novel, and it is the prelude to this exciting book series.

PRAISE FOR BARRACUDA

"In Barracuda: The Fate Diamond Series Book 3, authors Maury K. Downs and Lorna Downs delve into the mystical allure of the Almasi Ya Kifo diamonds, once a cherished charm for the main character, Paulo. However, as Paulo parts with these diamonds, a series of peculiar and unsettling events unfold, leading him to reconsider his decision. This tale, marked by a blend of suspense and the supernatural, follows Paulo's journey through a life increasingly dominated by misfortune and desperation.

The narrative is skillfully crafted, with meticulous attention to detail evident throughout the book. The portrayal of Paulo is particularly compelling; he embodies both the protagonist and antagonist roles, capturing a sense of internal conflict that is both frustrating and fascinating for the reader. Witnessing Paulo's decline is akin to observing a tragic, inevitable disaster - it's captivating and emotionally stirring. An interesting aspect of the book is its use of a narrator. This choice effectively prevents confusion that might arise from a solely Paulo-centric viewpoint, offering readers a more comprehensive understanding of the unfolding events. The narrator's presence enriches the story, providing a multifaceted perspective that heightens the tension and drama surrounding Paulo's fate.

Initially, the story's pace may appear slow, but this deliberate approach allows for a gradual and more impactful revelation of the plot. The authors' technique of showing rather than telling adds depth to the narrative, engaging readers as the story evolves into a complex and intriguing web. The book's narrative style evokes a sense of nostalgia reminiscent of classic storytelling, making it an enjoyable and easy read. Remarkably, Barracuda: The Fate Diamond Series Book 3 stands alone well, even as part of a series, inviting new readers without requiring them to have read the previous installments.

This book is a well-crafted blend of intrigue, suspense, and mystery. It appeals to a broad audience, transcends age barriers, and subtly offers insightful life lessons woven into its narrative. Barracuda is a commendable addition to the series and a worthwhile read for suspenseful and mystical storytelling fans." — *Literary Titan*

THE LEGEND OF THE ALMASI YA KIFO DIAMONDS

Legend has it the Almasi Ya Kifo diamonds were discovered in Africa. Although, the exact origin is unknown. The supernatural powers of the diamonds are the compelling conversations of legend and cultural folklore. The animate power of the cosmos within the diamonds amplifies all the harmonic energy of the possessor. For example, the generous intentions of a kind-hearted person's goodwill can be intensified, protecting them from harm and positively affecting others around them. Conversely, individuals disreputable in character will find pronounced misfortune along their path while in custody of the stones. Especially if there is any malicious intent, such as the exploitation of the gems for greed or selfish covetousness.

In diverse cultures the mysterious gems are known as "Fate Diamonds" because of the wealth and good luck they are said to bestow. Although they can bring good luck, the diamonds are legendarily known for the peculiar misgivings and calamities that follow when possessing them. Hence, their notorious epithet, Almasi Ya Kifo. A lingo in Swahili meaning, "Death Diamonds". Nevertheless, the diamonds are considered priceless by many experts in the diamond industry. The gems are so rare and the legend such a mystique, that they are tirelessly sought after by many gem collectors – and those with greedy intent.

Certain ancient tribes around the world acknowledge that the diamonds hold supernatural powers and retain an energy beyond any comprehension. These are the tribes that have a profound belief regarding the danger of the stones. They are people sworn under armistice and primed through ritual to keep the stones safely hidden when they fall in their possession at any given time.

Myth or fact, magic or science? This can only be determined by the individual experiencing the diamond's intense affects when in their possession.

CHAPTER 1
I WONDER WHERE MY LUCKY DIAMONDS ARE RIGHT NOW?

Saturday, September 29, 2001

IT'S A TYPICAL hot and sunny afternoon outside on the Las Vegas Strip. Though, Paulo Pineda is quite comfortable. Paulo is sitting inside the plush and colorful Tropicana Las Vegas lobby. The air conditioning inside the huge resort is ideal, nice and cool. He reads the Las Vegas Sun newspaper while patiently waiting for his club deluxe room to be ready.

Paulo is the type of young man incessantly seeking quick fortune. He is an avid gambler who frequents casinos, such as here in Las Vegas more often than he probably should. He is particularly enthusiastic about joining any multilevel marketing gimmick, no matter how risky the scheme may seem. Although a bit withdrawn, he is hasty to seize an opportunity if he thinks it is profitable for him, sometimes to the point of ignorant irresponsibility.

It's crowded. All around him are vacationers and tourists, talking aloud and meandering about. In the near distance, he hears the melodic jingles of slot machines, calling him like a Siren. However, Paulo ignores the beckoning songs of the wagering machines, for now. *There will be plenty of time for that later.* What Paulo needs right now, is a nice long nap. He has had a hectic, eventful Saturday.

· · · · ● · · ·

PAULO WAS BUSY earlier today at Los Angeles International Airport carrying out a meticulous plan his aunt Elvie had cleverly devised. Elvie trades diamonds and other precious gemstones around the world. She is considered an expert by many of her industry associates. As part of her business, she has trusted people that help her secretly get expensive valuables in and out of the country. Today's plan had involved Paulo stashing his precious Almasi Ya Kifo diamonds inconspicuously along with a coincident jewelry transporting job that was taking place.

Paulo had agreed for Elvie to help him get rid of the Almasi Ya Kifo diamonds. Why? So that Paulo could rid himself of the stone's legendary curse. When he had unexpectedly come into possession of the diamonds, he had experienced very strange and disturbing happenings.

Elvie's plan had all transpired without a hitch, almost. Unfortunately, while hastily trying to execute the plan, Paulo had accidentally smacked right into the beautiful transporter. The impact was solid enough to stir up a few gasps from some of the people sitting there at the departure gate. The young lady had fallen to the floor. Her purse, cell phone, and other belongings all strewn about on the floor.

The transporter knocked to the floor just happened to be Xenyatta Davenport, a successful fashion model with a secret freelance side profession. Xenyatta, Xen as her friends know her, was covertly carrying some priceless diamonds for a private insurance company.

Luckily, Paulo had been able to take advantage of the precarious opportunity. Nonchalantly and unobserved, he had placed his black velvet case of diamonds inside Xen's tote bag, on top of another case of diamonds she had been contracted to carry.

Paulo had sincerely apologized for his clumsiness. Luckily, neither of them was injured. He helped Xen stand to her feet. It was quite an embarrassing moment. Nevertheless, they had shared a kind smile.

Xen had assured Paulo that she was okay, content that everything was fine. What she hadn't realized is that an extra case of diamonds was in her possession. Paulo had successfully stashed the cursed Almasi Ya Kifo stones with her.

Xen boarded the flight with the other passengers. The door to the jetway closed. The United Airlines Boeing 747 pushed off the gate, right on schedule. As the aircraft slowly moved away, Paulo walked close to the large terminal windows. He watched the beautiful jumbo jet taxi and takeoff, headed for Italy.

Then Paulo took his flight to Las Vegas.

· · · · **·** · · ·

INSIDE THE TROPICANA lobby, Paulo stretches and yawns. He shakes his head and rolls his eyes, recalling how he clumsily smacked right into the pretty blonde transporter, bumping her off her feet. *Glad she was okay. And she never saw me place the diamonds in her purse.*

Yes indeed, Paulo needs a breather. He quietly turns the pages of the newspaper and starts to read an article about the Aladdin Resort, located nearby. He reads about the resort having some financial troubles of late.

"Mr. Pineda." Suddenly, the front desk lady calls out his name. "Sir, your room is ready now." She smiles as Paulo gets up and approaches her. "We apologize for the wait." She hands him the room key.

"Oh, that's okay." Paulo smiles in return.

"It's been so busy with Elton John being in town."

"Oh." Paulo recalls seeing the iconic artist's face glowing on the MGM Grand's gigantic digital marquee across the street.

Paulo makes his way through the crowd of people checking into the hotel and walks to the elevators. There he finds more people standing around, some with luggage, others holding souvenir alcoholic drinks of some kind. He hears their conversations. Everyone is making plans to meet up and be somewhere tonight. Paulo also has somewhere to be later, as well. He smiles. He can't wait to see Karen tonight. Karen and Paulo have worked together at the Megabuster video store the past three years. Although she is his boss at work, they are very good friends. Paulo has been seriously admiring her for some time now.

Paulo makes his way to his room and settles in. After counting his money, $3,450 Paulo lies down to take a nap. He stares at the ceiling, thinking. *I wonder where my lucky diamonds are right now.*

CHAPTER 2
THEY'RE YOURS. YOU KEEP THEM NOW, KID

Paulo came into possession of the notorious Almasi Ya Kifo diamonds by fateful happenstance. There was a horrible automobile accident that occurred late one night, outside a small bar that Paulo was in.

The crash involved three guys that had been in the bar. There had been some sort of disagreement between them. One of the men sitting close to Paulo had suddenly pulled out a gun and coerced the other two men to leave with him. Paulo was so frightened he didn't know what to do. The strangers left together with the man holding the gun.

Next, Paulo and the bartender, the only remaining people inside the bar, suddenly heard the terrible accident. Paulo hurried outside. When he looked inside one of the vehicles, he saw the three men that had just walked out of the bar. Two of the men in the front seats, appeared to be deceased. Paulo noticed that the man laid out on the rear bench seat was still conscious and breathing. He was the man that had been holding the other two at gunpoint.

The bartender called 911. As the sounds of emergency first response vehicles were heard approaching, the scruffy looking stranger in the rear seat made an unusual request. He didn't ask Paulo to help him. Instead, he wanted Paulo take and keep something before the police arrived.

That stranger, a man named Joseph Ashe, had stolen the mysterious Almasi Ya Kifo diamonds from his business partner's Las Vegas store. Joseph had tried to make it look like the store was robbed and vandalized in the process. However, his greedy business associates were not easily fooled. They caught up with Joseph at the bar that night. Those were the other two men, lying motionless in the front seats of the wrecked sedan.

Paulo did as Joseph requested. He took a small black velvet case out of the man's backpack. Paulo opened the case, and he beheld the most beautiful diamonds he'd ever seen. Held in his clutch, were the priceless Almasi Ya Kifo gemstones, sparkling, mesmerizing. Paulo was immediately rapt.

It was Joseph's last desire to give the stones away, to Paulo. Joseph had said to him, "Take them! And they will bring you great fortune!" Paulo smiles, thinking about how fortunate he was to be there at the right time when Joseph gave them to him. The last thing Paulo remembered Joseph saying was "They're yours. You keep them now, kid."

CHAPTER 3
OKAY, READY FOR SOME ACTION

Several hours later, after having a restful nap, watching some TV, and eating dinner, Paulo is ready to enjoy the evening. He had specifically ordered room service and dined in his room as he didn't want to chance walking through the casino lobby to get food and see all the slots beckoning him to play. He was doing his best to resist being tempted to gamble too early. Paulo prefers to gamble late in the evening whenever he comes to Las Vegas. He feels, that is the best and most rewarding time. He is convinced that is the time when the slots are loose, when they are paying best.

Paulo looks at his full-length reflection in the mirror. He turns from side to side, wondering what impression Karen will have about his fashion selection. He is handsomely groomed and dressed well for the evening. He is wearing black leather Alfani Derby shoes, charcoal dress slacks with leather belt, and a burgundy long-sleeved collar shirt.

He tugs at his shirt and shiny gold belt buckle, and smiles as he speaks to his reflection "Okay, ready for some action." With cash filled wallet, room key, and cell phone tucked in his slacks, Paulo heads out for his rendezvous with Karen.

Almost 9 PM and it's still a warm 81°F outside right now. The evening is full of energy. It's electrifying. There are crowds of excited people walking about, talking and laughing aloud. They're all looking at the dazzling sights. The street corner is nearly lit up like daytime from shining resort signage and massive digital advertising displays all around. Paulo grins wide from ear to ear. *It's a perfect evening. It's time to go to the Rumjungle nightclub and meet Karen.* He wonders with curious anticipation what adventures the electrifying night will bring.

Paulo walks along the expansive Tropicana Boulevard pedestrian bridge, crossing over all the congested automobile traffic below. He notices the New York New York Hotel and Casino across the street corner. There are many people gathered around the resort taking pictures and looking at all the printed photographs of loved ones and various personal memorabilia placed about. The huge iconic resort casino has become a makeshift 911 memorial. Paulo is in absolute awe. He sees the impressive myriad of T-shirts and small quilts that have been decoratively draped together, hanging all around the surrounding resort gate. Paulo can hear the difference. On his side of the corner people are cheery and laughing. And around the New York New York resort, the gathering of people is somberly quiet.

Paulo takes the Excalibur to Mandalay Bay tram. As the enclosed tram quickly hums along the elevated track, Paulo is growing more nervous with anticipation on meeting up with Karen. The tram arrives at the Mandalay Bay Resort and Casino full of people. The nighttime crowd is different from the people rambling about during the daytime. Earlier in the day, Paulo observed many people walking around wearing comfortable T-shirts, shorts, and flip-flops. But nighttime in Las Vegas is party time. Everyone around Paulo is dressed up now. The tram doors slide wide open, and everyone scurries out.

Paulo enters the Mandalay Bay and walks through the crowded casino floor towards the Rumjungle nightclub. He hears the thump of the music well before he sees the club entrance. His hands are slightly sweaty. He's more nervous than usual to see Karen. Paulo has never been out with her in a social setting that didn't include just their friends and coworkers. He is suddenly feeling, somewhat out of his element, and he doesn't know what to say to her. Paulo tries to think. *Surely there is something interesting we can talk about.* He starts to tap his foot and bob his head to the music, to help appease the nervousness building inside him. Paulo is lacking confidence. *She's probably not even here. I never got a call from her.* He looks at all the other people standing in line, also waiting to get into the popular nightclub.

"Paulo." He hears his name called over the music coming from inside the club. Paulo looks towards the entrance and sees Karen, waving and smiling at him. She points at a booth near the entrance of the posh dance club. Paulo smiles and waves enthusiastically back. He's overjoyed now. He promptly pays the $15 cover charge with nervous anticipation and enters. *I'm here. Made it!*

"Hey Karen!" Paulo approaches the booth saying enthusiastically, "Nice to see you!"

"Hey Paulo!" Karen replies, smiling. "It's nice to see you, too. Glad you made it." She politely introduces her friends sitting with her, pointing at them each. "This is Anita, and this is Pamela." Karen's friends greet Paulo and motion for him to sit. He sits next to Karen as she tells him, "DJ Sumner Stemp, he's Pamela's friend."

"Huh?" Paulo is preoccupied by the closeness of his coworker, the boss lady, right now. This is a rousing moment. Karen is fashionably dressed tonight in a lovely baby blue cocktail dress. Her straight, long black hair with cherry highlights, falls appealingly just past her shoulders. A rare delight because Karen always wears her hair up in various bun styles at work. Paulo notices she is wearing a little makeup and some lip gloss this evening, which is also not typical. Her dark brown eyes, long black hair, and moist red lips in stark variation to her fair skin tone, is delectably alluring.

Karen is a lovely product of mixed ethnicity. Karen's mother is of Chinese American descent, born and raised in Sacramento, California. Karen's father is white. He was born and raised in the heartland, Springfield, Missouri.

She looks hot! Paulo gets butterflies. He shifts his gaze away quickly, trying not to gawk at Karen. But he wants to.

"The DJ." Karen reiterates, as she leans and lowers her head slightly forward to make direct eye contact with Paulo. "He's Pamela's friend."

Paulo doesn't look at her. "Uh-huh", he musters a nervous reply, "right, yeah, you mentioned that." Avoiding eye contact, he looks at the table.

"He plays a lot of stuff, hip hop, progressive techno, house music. You know, dance music. He gets a lot of gigs." Pamela affirms. She smiles sprightly at Paulo, and with a slight inquisitive inflection, Pamela says, "So, Karen here says you two work together."

"Uh, yes, we do." Paulo notices the ladies share a brief glance at each other. "I've been working with Karen for a couple years now. She's my boss." He nods. "We're friends."

"How nice." Pamela responds with amusement, "Well, nice to meet you, Paulo."

Just then, the server arrives at their booth table and offers a tray of watermelon shots for each of them sitting there. "Compliments of the DJ." The server divulges, as she lowers the small tray within convenient reach of each of them. The precise moment Anita, Pamela, Karen, and Paulo reach for a shot glass, the music tempo changes and the volume increases. The hit song Family Affair by Mary J. Blige starts bumping. They all look at each other, and down their shots.

"Woo-hoo!" Pamela gives a shout, raising both arms high towards the ceiling. "Time to get crunk, girlfriend!" She swiftly rises to her feet, already gyrating her hips before she's anywhere near the dance floor. Anita stands quickly and starts moving her hips in the same manner. She's pouting her lips and gesturing towards Paulo and Karen to follow her and Pamela.

"Let's go, Paulo." Karen leans in close to Paulo, her eyes wide with excitement. She playfully tugs at his arm, giggling.

"Sure!" Paulo says, looking like a little kid that's been asked if he'd like some candy.

Pamela leads the way, pointing to her DJ friend as they approach the dance floor. He acknowledges with a nod and wide grin. Pamela gives a shout, as they each step onto the crowded dance floor. Next, Pamela, Anita, and Karen surround Paulo, and they all start moving to the hip, thumping groove. Good thing Paulo spent a lot of time while growing up dancing with his cousins on every occasion at Filipino family dinners, karaoke parties, birthday parties, and such. Ironically, Paulo is very comfortable right now. Because he really enjoys singing karaoke and dancing.

. . . . ● . . .

CLOSE TO 3 AM just before the nightclub closes Anita, Pamela, Karen, and Paulo leave the Rumjungle. They'd had an enjoyable evening dancing to almost every song the DJ played. And they thoroughly enjoyed the watermelon shots the DJ kept sending to their table throughout the evening. As they walk towards the guest elevators of the Mandalay Bay, they laugh about all the clowning and cavorting carried on this evening. Pamela is the loudest of the group, cackling at every joke or slightest suggestive innuendo anybody makes. It's that time of night after the party when everything is funny.

Karen turns to Paulo, saying just under the level of the other women's boisterous laughter, "Meet you for lunch if you'd like, if you have time before your flight." Karen slows her pace behind Anita and Pamela, who are swaying a bit in their high heels.

"That would be awesome!" Paulo steps closer to her, trying his best to contain his elation and, not jump up and down like he's just won the lottery jackpot. Karen, the woman of his sincere admiration has just asked him to lunch. And it's not in the cramped breakroom at work. Paulo grins. *Totally awesome!*

"I think I'm drunk!" Pamela wobbles a bit. She lowers her head, snickering.

"No shit Sherlock, you're a genius." Anita puts an arm around her friend, supporting her as they meander closer towards the elevators. "When did you figure that out, toots?"

Anita and Pamela look squarely at each other and burst into laughter, almost falling.

"How about noon, at the Excalibur buffet?" Karen suggests to Paulo, chuckling at her friends. She is more sober than the other two.

"That's perfect!" Paulo replies, still grinning. "I'll be there looking for you, Karen."

"Okay then, see you there." Karen turns and gives Paulo a quick hug. "And thank you for coming here and meeting my friends." She presses the elevator button.

"Wait." Pamela, a bit slurred utters, "Did I bring the room key?" She looks serious.

"I have the other key." Karen assures, showing her the spare. "No worries."

Pamela looks around, astounded. Paulo casually notices that Pamela is holding her room key snug against the side of her small purse. Pamela had taken it out of her purse a few minutes ago. Pamela's eyes find Paulo looking at her now. He gestures with his eyes, nodding his chin at her. Pamela frowns at him, confused. Then, Pamela glances down, noticing she is holding the key. "Oh, I have it!" She raises her hand to show everyone proof. Pamela looks awestruck at Anita. The two inebriated ladies burst into boisterous laughter, again.

The elevator arrives with a sounding ding and the doors open. Karen gently pulls Pamela and Anita, still laughing, into the elevator car before the doors close. They all turn to Paulo, waving, each thanking him for an enjoyable evening. Paulo waves and wishes them well. Paulo looks at Karen. She smiles in return, looking directly at him as the elevator doors close.

Paulo has been having so much fun. The evening has simply been, terrific. This occasion was far less tense for him than he had imagined it would be. He got to spend time with Karen, without the usual mob of his juvenile coworkers being around. He enjoyed meeting Karen's friends. To Paulo, meeting Anita and Pamela made him feel very special. Karen is including him in her clique now. It's like high school, again. Paulo is hanging out with the cool kids. Karen has never asked Paulo to meet him anywhere, especially to go clubbing. Paulo is feeling like he is the luckiest man on earth right now.

"I think I'll try my luck at the slots, since I'm having such a good time." Paulo says to himself, nodding and rubbing his chin. "If only I still had my lucky diamonds."

CHAPTER 4
ZERO!

By 7:35 AM Paulo is munching on a glazed donut and drinking his third cup of black coffee. He sits quietly, staring at the Texas Tea video slot machine in front of him. Paulo is at the Golden Nugget downtown, on Fremont Street. The iconic casino is not crowded right now, allowing him plenty of choices to gamble. This is the third casino he has played slots in since leaving the nightclub last night. He tried his luck at the Luxor and the Stratosphere, but the slots just weren't lucratively paying. He sighs heavily, frustrated. Paulo has gambled away almost half the money he brought with him.

Paulo has an idea. Since the slots aren't paying, perhaps he should venture to the card tables. He looks around and searches for the nearest opportunity. He notices a blackjack table where one person, a young man is playing. After finishing the last bite of his donut, Paulo strides over there and takes a seat on the far right. The other player is seated in the middle. Paulo is eager to try his luck at the quiet card table. Paulo is all smiles.

The dealer wins seven hands in a row, with three of those being blackjack. The other player quits and leaves. But not Paulo. He stays, frequently using double down bets in hopes of turning his luck around. After a few hours go by playing a $10 minimum bet, it doesn't take Paulo much time to dwindle his cash.

Deciding to try his luck elsewhere, Paulo heads to the roulette table. He sits comfortably and greets the dealer. He is the only player at the table now. Paulo purchases chips and begins playing, putting $40 on red. The dealer spins the wheel and puts the ball into play. Paulo is having second thoughts about his bet on red just now.

As the brisk sound of the ball is heard rounding the ball track, the dealer waves her hand across the table, declaring, "No more bets." The ball hits one of the metal diamonds on the outer section of the wheel squarely, and it plops into the green zero pocket. Paulo hears solemn confirmation from the dealer. "Zero!"

"Awe man." Paulo responds, as he sulks in his chair. "I was gonna bet that one."

Paulo presses his luck, placing $60 on red, again. He also puts $50 worth of chips to cover his wager and increase his chances of winning on various inside bets. And as the little white ball launches into play, Paulo puts another $60 on zero.

"No more bets." The dealer says aloud, waving her arm across the table above the wagered chips. The ball whirls around the wheel.

Paulo watches fervently. Next, he hears and beholds the ball bounce and land snug in the green double zero pocket. His jaw drops in disbelief, absolutely astounded.

"Double zero!" The dealer declares, swiftly collecting all his losing bets.

"Man, I should have not given my lucky diamonds away. I really need them back." Paulo grumbles aloud, shaking his head regretfully.

The dealer hears Paulo. She glances at him for a second, perplexed. Then it's back to business. She raises her chin as if she were addressing a crowd. "Place your bets!"

Paulo continues to play over the next hour. He remains in his seat, mostly losing or breaking even at best on his wagers. Then, an elderly man stops by to try his luck. He greets everyone cheerfully as he takes a seat close to Paulo. The well-dressed man is holding a large black coffee. Paulo watches as the man pours what can only be assumed to be hard liquor from a silver flask into the hot beverage.

He winks at Paulo and laughs as he jests, "Breakfast of champions!"

Breakfast? Paulo suddenly remembers his lunch date with Karen. He pulls his cellphone out from his pocket, noticing the time, 11:24 AM. Realizing he is literally on the other side of town, Paulo decides he must leave now.

Paulo cashes in his scant remaining chips and leaves the Golden Nugget casino. He walks quickly to the public bus terminal nearby just in time to catch the next bus headed south down the strip. By the time he arrives at the Excalibur and walks the long distance inside to the buffet it is 12:11 PM. He sees Karen, standing by the buffet line, looking around. Her eyes find Paulo scurrying towards her. She smiles, brightly.

"Hey Karen!" Paulo says, almost out of breath from his vigorous walk through the huge casino. He manages to chuckle a bit.

"Hey you!" Karen greets him happily. "You hungry? I'm starved." She grins. "And, lunch is on me, Paulo. I'm the one who asked you to come, so my treat." She nods and pats him on the arm. "Is that okay?"

"Oh, are you sure?" Paulo asks courteously. Though he is quite relieved. Because Paulo is nearly broke now. He was just about to ask Karen if he could pay her back for his meal.

"Yes, now come on, let's eat." She gestures for them to enter the busy, popular buffet.

They're soon enjoying the most delicious meal together, relaxing and laughing about their previous evening at the dance club. Karen tells Paulo that Anita and Pamela had slept most of the morning. She says her friends had an earlier flight back to Los Angeles to catch and had left the hotel just before Paulo had arrived at the buffet. They wanted her to thank Paulo again for coming to meet them, and they also had a lot of fun.

Their conversation centers on humorous situations that have occurred at their workplace, Megabuster video store. Many of those amusing moments include their friend and coworker, Tommy, who's always up to something goofy. His nerdy demeanor has earned him an endearing nickname over the past couple years. Some of the employees called him Urkel for a while, in reference to the popular comedy character on television. Tommy could imitate that character pretty good, actually.

"So, are you still thinking about going to dental school?" Paulo changes the subject, taking an interest in Karen's future career plans. He is trying to sound more sophisticated now, after jesting about silly antics at work.

"Yes, I am." Karen replies. "I've got a few more classes and tests to take, before I can apply." She continues to eat some food on her plate.

Paulo stares at her for a moment, thinking. Then he asks, "Don't you have an uncle that works at the Pleasant Hills Dental School? Something like that, right?"

Karen smiles. "My aunt Joyce." She wipes her mouth and continues. "She is one of the associate clinical professors there. Yes."

"Nice!" Paulo is nodding, "You got a way in, yea?"

They chuckle as Karen shakes her head, "Well, I don't know about that. She always tells me to keep studying. She really encourages me." Karen says humbly. "But yeah, I'm like her favorite niece, because I want to do what she does."

"Nice!" Paulo continues nodding playfully, wide eyed. They chuckle again.

"So," Karen quickly changes the subject, "doesn't your mom work at Pleasant Hills? She's a nurse, right?"

"Yes." Paulo confirms. "She loves it."

"Is that something you've thought of doing, you know, becoming a registered nurse?"

"Who me?" Paulo grimaces. "Oh no. I get nauseated at the sight of blood."

"Really?" Karen is genuinely surprised.

"My mom and dad really wanted me to go to nursing school and become a nurse a few years ago. But nah." Paulo, shaking his head. "It's not for me. I'm not interested."

He shrugs his shoulders and continues eating. There is a moment of quiet. Then, Karen asks an interesting question.

"Hey, was your mom working that special day?" Paulo tilts his head out of curiosity as Karen says, "You know, at the hospital."

"What?"

"About three weeks ago?" She is deadpan serious. "You know, the miracle."

"Oh, that." Paulo recalls what happened and what his mother had told him. "Yeah, she said it was really weird. She thinks it was a miracle, too." Paulo shrugs and winces. "Yeah, but you know." He looks down at his plate, stirring some steamed rice and teriyaki chicken with his fork. He thinks of what more he has to say about it. He had heard and seen it all on the news, as many other people had. "I don't know, man."

They are talking about a peculiar happening that occurred at Pleasant Hills Medical Center some weeks ago. Early one morning, all the patients in the hospital spontaneously recovered from whatever diagnosis or ailment they were admitted for. Every patient. The event caught global attention, airing on local and international news for several days.

"Every sick person in the entire hospital was like, suddenly better. All of a sudden, people were just, healed." Karen replies, astonished in recollection of what had happened. "I heard a rumor it started in the children wards first."

"Yeah, that's what I heard." Paulo acknowledges with raised speculative eyebrows.

"It was all over the news." Karen continues, "To this day there are still small crowds of people who come just to see the hospital and take pictures outside and, hold up signs and stuff. I remember the huge crowds and all the people honking their horns in their cars a few days after it happened." Karen pauses, then says, "It's quietened down since, you know, the terrorist attacks and all. But things were pretty lively there for a while."

"I know." Paulo replies, "I remember going there to get some lunch money from my mom when she was working and, seeing all the crazy people. They all chanting, 'miracle-hospital, miracle-hospital' and that kind of stuff." Paulo, waving his hand dismissively, "Crazy."

"You…" Karen hesitates. "You don't think it was a miracle?"

"Well," Paulo sighs as he poses his reply, "I read that it was just a very unusual circumstance kind of thing. You, know. It's like, the odds of something like that happening was much less than lightning striking you. But it's possible. And it was just, one of those times, or something like that. It was a very scientific article I read." Paulo nods assuredly.

"Well, I'm not the holiest person around. I mean, I go to church on Easter and stuff. But I do think there may have been some divine intervention happening there somewhere." Karen gestures. "I don't know."

"Yeah, I don't know." Paulo smirks. "But whatever, I guess." He looks at his phone, curious of the time. "I'm having fun, Karen. But it looks like we should be heading to the airport soon?"

Karen agrees it is time to go and they make arrangement to share a cab to the airport. As they prepare to leave, Paulo tells Karen that he will leave the gratuity for their server. No sooner than they get up, and after Karen turns to walk away, Paulo has second thoughts. He wants to keep the cash. He snatches the tip he'd placed from their table and hastily stuffs the money into his pocket again, before Karen can notice.

· · · • · · ·

As soon as their cab leaves the Excalibur, Paulo asks Karen a question.

"Hey, Karen. Can I ask you something?"

"Yes, Paulo, what is it?" Karen looks into Paulo's eyes, with slight charming smile.

"You think I can pay you back for the cab? I'm a little short on cash right now."

"No problem." Karen casually reassures. "I got it. No need to pay me back."

"Thanks." Paulo is relieved she was so willing to pay. He is much more relaxed now. The nervousness and anxiety he used to feel being around Karen has greatly diminished, after spending some time together. Then Paulo gets another idea. She might be able to make him some money. And she could benefit from it, too. "Hey, Karen."

"Yes?" Her soft-spoken response is followed by a look into his eyes again.

"How would you like to make some extra cash?"

"Huh?" She looks at him, puzzled.

Paulo goes on to tell her about his many, industrious money ventures. He talks about how he made money playing an airplane game. He tries to sound convincing, telling her she needs to join the next cruise ship game that is just beginning. He insists it is important she joins now, while the game is just starting. Then, Paulo talks about his other extra income opportunities, like Amway, Herbalife, and such. Paulo is very surprised to hear that she is not involved in any of those ventures. Nevertheless, Karen tells him they're just not for her.

The entire time he is talking, Karen realizes something is different about Paulo. He is acting pushy, almost to the point of being demanding that she join something and pay. He keeps telling her, they can both benefit from her participation in his ventures, and she is missing out.

What Karen doesn't realize is the reason why Paulo seems

so different as of late. She has no idea that Paulo once had in his possession, the rarest of all diamonds on the planet. But they weren't just any conventional, priceless diamonds. If Karen only knew the mysterious cosmic influence and unquantifiable energy the gemstones retain, she would certainly understand. Her dear friend, Paulo has become completely consumed by his greed. Paulo's circumstance is a unique one. A most peculiar lingering effect of the bewitching, Almasi Ya Kifo diamonds.

They arrive at McCarran International Airport and make their way to the security screening. While going through the metal detectors, Paulo and Karen hear some people talk about the extra time it takes now to get through screening, and how things have changed. A couple of security officers start talking about a new national airport security and screening system that will be coming from the US Department of Transportation, very soon. Most definitely, the screening process will become a completely different experience, they hear the security officers declare.

After passing through the screening, Karen tells Paulo about a concert she wants to attend. She wonders if he and Tommy might be interested. She tells him it is the Bridge School Benefit 2001, which will take place at the Shoreline Amphitheatre in Mountain View, California. Some of her favorite music artists will perform at the venue, R.E.M., Pearl Jam, Tracy Chapman, Neil Young and Crazy Horse, Billy Idol, Dave Matthews, Ben Harper, and Jill Sobule. Karen has close family in San Jose, California. She offers him and Tommy to stay with her at her cousin's house. Paulo expresses his sincere interest and assures her he will let Tommy know. Paulo is thrilled. *Wow! Hanging with the cool kids now.*

Karen's America West flight departs before Paulo's Southwest flight on the other side of the terminal. But Paulo has just enough time to walk Karen to her departure gate, to see her off. Before she leaves, she gives him a tender hug, and a pleasant kiss on his cheek. A simple gesture of affection. But it is practically all Paulo thinks about on the way to his gate and the flight back home.

CHAPTER 5
NO THANKS DUDE

Paulo arrives in Los Angeles and has just enough cash to pay the parking garage fee where he had left his car. After paying, he now has $9 left from the $3,450 he took with him on the trip to Las Vegas. Glancing at his gas gauge, Paulo sees he has enough for the drive back home. He planned it that way. He smiles. Then he thinks how much money he would have returned with if his lucky diamonds had been with him on the trip.

"That is what I originally planned, before I let Elvie scare me into giving them away." Paulo says aloud. "I need to call her. I wonder if she can find them and get them back." Paulo considers, knowing if Elvie can find that kind of information out. *I bet if she stops talking about them being cursed and stuff, I can keep having my good luck. Maybe she was the reason I was having the bad luck, after all.* Paulo nods. "Yeah, I bet."

Paulo stops by his coworker's apartment to tell him about his eventful weekend. Tommy is happy to see him and welcomes his friend inside. They begin to play another one of Tommy's brand-new video games he got for his new PlayStation 2.

"Dude, let's play this new Madden football game I got from our store." Tommy says, reaching for the game controllers. "It's the best game." He shows Paulo the 'Madden NFL 2001' game case with Tennessee Titans running back Eddie George and John Madden picture logo on the front cover.

"Sure." Paulo smiles and sits comfortably down.

Paulo tells Tommy about the upcoming concert that Karen mentioned, and they agree to go together. While they enjoy playing, Paulo suggests they order pizza. Tommy thinks that is a great idea for dinner and he places an order on the phone. Paulo says he'll pay Tommy back.

Next, Paulo gets a call on his cell phone. "Hello." Paulo answers, as Tommy pauses the game. "Hey, Jacqueline." Paulo continues talking to his friend regarding the next multilevel wagering gimmick he wants to participate in.

Listening to Paulo, Tommy has a good idea what the conversation is about.

Jacqueline tells Paulo the new cruise ship game is about to begin, and the entry 'investment' will be $100 this time. The stakes are higher now because the last airline game was so popular.

"Oh yeah, I'm definitely in." Paulo grins. He can't wait to start playing. Tommy is shaking his head right now.

"Very nice!" Paulo replies. He enjoyed making extra cash from the last scheme. He ends the call, rubbing his hands vigorously together, like he's just sealed a million-dollar deal on something significant. But Tommy already knows it's a game that takes advantage of players joining later. Those who make a wager soon after other participants have, are already at a great disadvantage. Basically, it is just another Ponzi scheme.

"Let me guess." Tommy figures, "Was that your nurse friend playing that airline game?"

"Yes, that was Jacqueline." Paulo snaps his finger and points at his friend. "Hey, you should play this time. I'm serious. Play our cruise ship game and make money like I did last game."

"Dude, you sound so Filipino right now, just like your dad." Tommy chuckles.

"I don't sound like my dad."

"Yeah, when you get excited, you do." Tommy stares at his friend with a playful smirk.

"Whatever." Paulo waves his hand.

"Anyway, no thanks dude." Tommy replies.

They continue playing the video game and enjoy the pizza when it arrives. After several hours go by, Paulo figures it's time to leave. Before Paulo goes home, he asks Tommy for gas money. He tells Tommy that Vegas was not paying like he thought it would, and he was a little short on cash right now. But at least he had a great time meeting up with Karen and her friends. Tommy is happy for him. He gives Paulo some cash.

By the time Paulo gets home his parents are already asleep. He heads upstairs to his room quietly as not to disturb them. He changes for bed and lies down. Paulo thinks of the wonderful weekend he just enjoyed. He and Karen are really getting to know each other better. *Things are looking good.* Paulo is feeling a little more confident about their blossoming friendship now.

Paulo thinks again about what the Las Vegas weekend would have been like if he had those beautiful diamonds. He closes his eyes and wishes he had them again.

CHAPTER 6
WHEN ARE YOU GONNA PAY UP, MAN?

The next day at work, Monday, October 1

Paulo is having a good day at Megabuster. Tommy and Karen are also working today. His friends are their usual lively selves, making the day go by with lighthearted humor. They genuinely enjoy working together. During Karen's lunchbreak, Paulo sits for a few minutes at the breakroom table. He tells Karen he and Tommy will go to the upcoming concert. Paulo asks if she can cover him for the cost of the tickets. He mentions he will repay her this week. Karen tells him it's not a problem, and he can pay her back anytime. Paulo is very grateful, and promises to pay her back, soon. When he asks if he wants her to collect Tommy's half of the money, Karen replies, saying Tommy has already paid her.

Paulo asks her again if she wants in on the cruise ship game. She declines. *He'll get someone else*, he thinks. As Paulo leaves the breakroom, he immediately recognizes a mutual friend of his and Tommy inside the store. The gentleman is there to rent a new video. Paulo recruits him to join the cruise ship game. Soon after, through casual conversation Paulo convinces another frequent patron of the store to join the game.

Tommy's father, Raymond stops by the store after ending his shift at San Bernardino County Fire Station 226. He is looking at new movies on the shelf to rent when Paulo notices him. Paulo almost convinces him to join. However, firefighter Raymond quickly changes his mind when he notices Tommy making adamant silent gestures not to participate. Tommy is poking his head around an isle corner behind Paulo, shaking his head and making faces at his dad. His dad got the message.

· · · • • • · ·

AFTER WORK, PAULO drives to his favorite local comics bookstore, Fantasy Comix. The store is situated along Mainstreet in the nearby quaint City of Redlands. The store clerk greets him cheerfully, welcoming Paulo back. It's been a few weeks since Paulo last visited the small store. Paulo takes his time trying to find editions he can add to his growing collection of illustrated periodicals. As he peruses the filled isles of previously owned comics, Paulo finds something in particular that he is looking for. It is the missing edition of his Suicide Squad DC comics collection.

"Whoa!" Paulo remarks, as he picks the comic up and inspects it closely. It is Volume 1, January 1991, Issue #49, "Out of Control", on sale for $7 almost new.

"Looks like you found something." The young store clerk smiles at Paulo. "Somebody was looking at that today. And I think that's the only one we have in the store."

"Yeah, lucky me." Paulo responds to the clerk behind the register. He flips through the pages and inspects the back and front cover again. "Out of Control." Paulo reads the title, suddenly realizing something that charismatically reminds him of his dear aunt Elvie. The cover art depicts an angry woman seated in a wheelchair, brandishing a large, scoped revolver.

"Auntie!" Paulo chuckles to himself.

He remembers hearing from his father, many stories about Elvie's audacious deeds from back in her day. Paulo's father refers to Elvie as being nothing more than a swanky hoodlum, when discussions about her come up in family conversations. His dad says she was always armed with a gun, and she probably still is. Paulo shakes his head and chuckles again. *I can't picture her like that. Elvie? Nah.*

Deciding it is time to go home for dinner now, Paulo purchases the comic. As Paulo walks out of the store, three nerdy teenage boys dressed up Punk follow close behind him. They were patiently waiting for him to exit the store. They were lucky to find him there. As Paulo reaches his car, he hears his name called from behind him.

"Yo, Paulo." The oldest of the group speaks up. Paulo turns around.

"Johnny Babcock." Paulo smiles. "How are you doing? What can I do for you?" Paulo recognizes the boys from around the neighborhood. Johnny and his family are also parishioners at the same Catholic Church that Paulo's mother attends. Standing close to Johnny are his geeky friends, Kevin Green and Louis Park.

"When are you gonna pay up, man?" The slim teenager queries bluntly. He wants to know when Paulo is going to pay his little sister back. Paulo never paid for some Girl Scout cookies several months ago. Their mom had to cover the expense and pay the money Paulo was supposed to give for two boxes of Samoas.

"Huh?" Paulo chuckles, smirking.

"Yeah, man." Johnny points at Paulo, saying, "My sister Leah sold you some Girl Scout cookies, dude. Remember? You owe her eight bucks, man." Johnny is serious. He and his friends try to look tough, but the sight of them standing so nerdy and close together makes Paulo start to giggle. The teenagers look at each other, perplexed for a second.

"Yeah, okay." Paulo waves his hand airily. "I will pay her. I will stop by your house and drop off the money."

"Okay man." Johnny replies, nodding confidently. "Cool."

The teenagers look at each other again, and they turn to leave.

Paulo gets in his car and drives away chuckling, as the nerdy Punk boys saunter off.

· · · · **·** · · ·

WHEN PAULO ARRIVES home, he notices his dad's car is not there when he pulls in. "Oh, that's right, it's Monday night football. I'm sure dad is with his buddies watching the game." He says to himself.

Paulo's father, Alejo loves Monday night football. Alejo never misses participating in his coworker Monday Night NFL pool. Paulo remembers hearing his father is betting on the San Francisco 49ers to win against New York Jets tonight.

This is an opportune moment. Paulo is happy his dad is not home, so he can have some time to talk to his mom alone. As soon as he walks through the front door, Paulo sees his mom sitting quietly at the dining room table.

"Hey mom what are you doing?" Paulo greets his dear mother.

"Oh, hey anak (*son*). I'm doing some inventory of my Amway and Avon." Mary replies.

"I see." Paulo walks over to the table, looking curiously at paperwork, various merchandise, and other products placed about.

"I have been very busy lately at the hospital and by the time I get home I'm tired to do anything. Do you want to join me for dinner since your dad is not here?" Mary smiles, while setting a small box of premium lipstick on the table. She glances at him over her reading glasses.

"Sure Mom. But let me take a quick shower. I'll be down shortly."

Mary clears up her clutter and sets the table nicely for their meal. Next, she walks into the kitchen and prepares their plates with the food she just cooked. Paulo soon returns downstairs. He is so appreciative of his mom when he joins her at the dinner table. They have a nice conversation about his trip to Las Vegas. He tells his mom he had a great time with Karen and her friends. Though, he doesn't mention gambling all night. He neglects telling his mother he lost all his money and, how he barely made it back home.

Paulo talks with his mother about all his money ventures. He insistently tells her that she should join the investment opportunities he is undertaking. He is assertive of the profitability she will have if she participates. Mary is excited to hear it all. Beyond any doubt, she is so proud of her son. She really wants to join every venture. However, Amway and Avon keep her busy enough these days. Not to mention her full-time nursing job at Pleasant Hills Medical Center.

"Maybe next time. I barely have time for myself these days." She replies.

"Come on Mom, we will do it together! I will help you." Paulo insists encouragingly, clasping his hands together.

"Paulo, I said next time." Mary firmly replies with a pronounced nod.

"Well okay, fine." Paulo settles his sales pitch tone down just a bit, "And since you don't want to join, can I borrow two hundred dollars then? I am going to try the new cruise ship game."

Mary looks at her son in disbelief. "Are you serious? Is that why you want me to join, to pay for you?"

"No, no, no. I am expecting money to come, but it's not going to be here in time for this game. I will pay you as soon as I get it next week." Paulo says assuredly.

With a heavy sigh, Mary agrees to lend her son the $200. She gives him all the cash in her purse, $90 for now. Then tells him she will leave more money in his room tomorrow. Paulo thanks his mom for the money and their time eating together. He stands up from his seat at the dinner table and takes his plate to the kitchen. Paulo helps his mother clean up the table and takes the trash out. When he returns, Paulo sees his mom is about to go upstairs to her bedroom. Paulo kisses her cheek and walks behind her upstairs. Mary is planning to go to bed soon. But Paulo is planning to leave for the Native American Casino in Coachella, after she falls asleep.

· · · · • · · ·

A LITTLE PAST midnight, Tuesday, October 2

Paulo is frustrated. He sits quietly in front of the Jackpot Party video slot machine he is playing, staring at the animated display reels. Paulo's gambling effort has yielded him zero profit tonight. The shiny wagering machines are basically paying back what he puts into them, back and forth, breaking even. Paulo sighs.

At that moment, a woman sits next to him at the adjacent slot machine. She inserts $20 into the money bezel and makes herself comfortable. Paulo is watching her. She begins playing, activating a scatter symbol free spin bonus on her first attempt. As the Jackpot Party jingle plays during the free spin, the woman smiles and dances to the tune. The woman is well dressed, full figured and very attractive. Paulo notices her wedding ring. It is a beautifully set, one carat diamond solitaire. Paulo sighs again. *My diamonds were way more beautiful than that one. Worth more than a thousand of those!*

"I wish I had them back." Paulo desires aloud.

The woman turns to look at him for a second. She promptly returns her attention to opening the tantalizing row of party doors displayed. Paulo is staring at the woman's diamond ring. He can almost sense it right now. The coaxing lure of the Almasi Ya Kifo gemstones. A feeling similar to the salutation of a suggestive whisper, charming him whenever he looked at them. Paulo is hexed, consumed by the unquenchable wanting. He must have them. He is more certain he can control them next time. *If I only had another chance.*

Paulo decides it is time to leave. He stops at a 24-hour fast food restaurant that is conveniently adjacent to the busy casino. The dining area is still open. There are a few people there, quietly enjoying their food. He chooses to eat inside. Paulo gets a combination hamburger meal with large fries and a large A&W Root Beer to satisfy his appetite. The salty savory aroma of the freshly made hot fries make him realize he is hungrier than he had anticipated. He takes his order and sits at a booth next to the window.

"Paulo Pineda?"

Paulo is startled. He turns and looks up at an elderly gentleman who is standing right next to his booth. Paulo grimaces. He thinks he recognizes the man, but Paulo can't quite remember the occasion. Paulo takes a generous sip of his ice-cold root beer through the tall narrow drinking straw while he thinks about it.

"You're Paulo Pineda, aren't ya?" The elderly man enquiries frankly.

"Yes sir." Paulo replies, placing his drink on the table. Paulo reaches for some hot fries as the gentleman stares down at him. He still can't remember where he met this old man before.

"I'm Harold Bishop, and that's my wife, Shirley." The gentleman points behind him toward a nearby table. There's an elderly woman sitting there. She smiles at Paulo and waves at him. Harold, not smiling, stares at Paulo again.

"How can I help you sir?" Paulo asks politely, while opening a packet of ketchup.

"My wife bought some vitamins and minerals from you a while back." Harold brushes his nose with his thumb and postures a bit, looking sterner now.

"Yeah? Okay." Paulo raises his eyebrow. "Must have been from my Herbalife." He leans back and looks at the man. "You want more vitamins, sir?"

"We never got them!" Harold puts his hands on his hips. He is growing angrier. "We called and left messages, but you never returned our calls. We've been waiting for several months for our order now. But now that I found you here, I'll just ask for my money back!"

Paulo suddenly remembers the man and his wife. Shirley owns a small hobby store in Palm Springs. Paulo went into the store one day and struck up a conversation, which eventually led to a sale of his Herbalife merchandise. He sold them a supply of vitamins and minerals, and Paulo promised to send the merchandise to them. However, Paulo needed the cash at the time, and he kept the money. He forgot to settle their $57 order. That was almost three months ago. Paulo rubs his chin, contemplating an agreeable compromise.

"Tell you what." Paulo pouts, thinking. "I can deliver you the order and I can include some perfume bath soap. I'll only charge half price for the additional soap order. How about that?" He smiles at the old man.

"How about I give you a knuckle sandwich young man?!" Harold is wide-eyed, pointing a finger at Paulo's face. "You're cruisin' for a bruisin' mister!" The elderly man flexes his limp muscles. "You're lucky I'm not the sailor boy I used to be at your age."

"Harold, that's enough!" Shirley pushes her tall, lean husband to get his attention. She had swiftly ambled over there from their nearby table. "Leave him alone, he doesn't have the merchandise now. He will remember to send it. Right?" She looks encouragingly at Paulo.

"Yeah, sure." Paulo responds, coolly. "I will send it."

"There, see?" Shirley looks at her husband, rubbing his long, skinny arm. "It's going to be okay, dear. The young man says he will send it." She nods reassuringly at Harold. Then she looks at Paulo. "You have to excuse my dear Harold. He still thinks he's quite the rough and tough sailor man." She chuckles, embarrassingly.

"If you don't deliver, well, you just better never step foot in our store again mister, or else!" Harold scoffs at Paulo, showing the young man a scrawny fist, nodding.

"Or…" Paulo, ignoring the warning, has another resourceful idea, "I can enroll you into my exclusive cruise ship game, with a chance to win several times the money you invest. All I need is an additional forty dollars. I'll give you a discount deal." Paulo nods, smiling again.

"Whuh…" Harold, eyes wide open in disbelief at the preposterous notion. He grabs at Paulo's shirt and tries to shove Paulo into the booth, almost stumbling in the process. Shirley pulls her husband's arm, trying to help keep him from falling over.

"Harold! Stop that right now!" Shirley is much shorter, but the stocky woman is clearly strong enough to pull her husband away.

By this time, the restaurant manager appears from behind the front counter. He speaks up, clearly. "What's the problem here? This is a peaceful establishment, please. Do I need to call the cops?"

Harold and Shirley say nothing more. They look at each other and walk swiftly out the glass door exit, arm in arm. Next, the chubby, oversized glasses wearing manager stares at Paulo for a second. Paulo says nothing. Paulo tugs on his shirt to straighten it out, then he nonchalantly picks up his burger and takes a big bite. The manager quietly walks away.

CHAPTER 7
DUDE, HE DOESN'T HAVE A CAT!

Wednesday, October 3

Paulo sits quietly, crunching on his favorite order of Taco Supremes from Taco Bell. Tommy made the lunch run earlier, surprising his best friend Paulo with the food. While Paulo eats, Karen walks into the small breakroom.

"Hey, Paulo, mind if I join you?" Karen smiles, retrieving her lunch container of leftover home cooking and a bottled water from the breakroom refrigerator.

"Oh, hey." Paulo motions for Karen to sit with him, Diet Pepsi in hand. "Please, do."

It has been a busy morning. The two have barely had time to speak. Paulo has been working the front register for most of the day. Paulo is happy to see that Karen has decided to join him for lunch. He watches her warm her food in the microwave.

"What do you have today?" Paulo raises his eyebrows, peering inquisitively at her food.

"Nothing special. Some leftover eggplant parmesan and salad." Karen smiles, as she sits at the small lunch table.

"Ooh," Paulo jests, "healthy, yeah?" They both chuckle.

Paulo clears his throat and takes a sip of his drink. He is much more relaxed than he used to be whenever Karen talks with him now.

But Paulo is still uncertain how to pursue a serious relationship with her. Moreover, he still lacks confidence. He is comfortable with their developing friendship for now. Perhaps he will ask her out soon. Paulo considers that's a reasonable possibility.

"Hey Paulo, would you like to go to Santa Monica this Sunday and see a local group? They're called California Calistoga. I think the band is really from Calistoga." Karen nods, fork in hand. "I really like them. It'll be great." She begins eating her salad.

"Uh…" Paulo is stunned. He is so surprised Karen is asking him out, he doesn't know how to respond. "… local band?" It's all he can put together. He stares at her.

"They sing alternative rock and some other stuff. They're awesome." Karen replies.

Paulo had considered the invitation to join Karen in Las Vegas to meet her friends was a friendly, casual gesture. Tommy was supposed to go, but his friend had to work last weekend. Now, Paulo is being asked out, on what appears to be a genuine date with Karen.

"That's awesome, yes, I want to go." Paulo's voice almost cracks with enthusiasm.

Karen, hearing his eager reply, smiles a bit. "Great."

She tells Paulo the band is performing this coming Sunday, October 7, at 4 PM at the Red Onion in Santa Monica. Paulo is delighted. He is looking forward to going with Karen to see the band perform. And while they are on the topic of concerts, Paulo promises he will pay her back for the tickets to the Bridge View concert, happening in a few weeks. Paulo says he is waiting for his upcoming Friday paycheck. Karen assures him not to worry, and she will take care of their food when they go to the beach city area this weekend. Paulo offers to drive.

· · · · • ● • · · ·

Leaving work, Paulo decides to drive over to Fantasy Comix. The same store clerk is working, greeting Paulo and welcoming him back. Paulo walks around, looking for more editions he can add to his collection. In the process, Paulo strikes up a conversation with the clerk and talks excitedly to him about the cruise ship game. He convinces the store clerk to join. The young man gives Paulo the $100 entry fee, all the cash he has.

Paulo buys a DC collectable Robin action figure for his computer desk at home. It will complement his Batman figurine, perfectly. Paulo says goodbye to the store clerk and exits the comics store. Johnny, Kevin, and Louis are sitting on a parking curb in an empty slot right next to Paulo's car. The spiked hair, fingerless glove wearing, Punk fashioned teenagers stand up when Paulo notices them.

"Johnny Babcock." Paulo grins, thinking how the boys all look like a 1980s Billy Idol music video gone bad. He wants to chuckle. But Paulo keeps his composure, asking politely, "What can I do for you guys?"

The boys look at each other. Then Johnny speaks up, coolly composed.

"My sister is still waiting for the money, dude."

"Johnny," Paulo replies sincerely, "I will stop by next week. Okay?"

"Okay. It's all good." Johnny straightens his posture a bit and gestures with gloved hand. "I'm just making sure we understand each other, dude."

Johnny taps Kevin with the back of his hand without looking at him. Kevin gestures, doing the same, tapping Louis with the back of his gloved hand. Paulo stares out of curiosity as the skinny Korean kid, Louis quickly reaches behind the group and produces a small pet carrier. As the portable kennel comes into full view, Paulo sees something moving inside.

Next, Paulo hears the distinct meow of a cat. He peers into the carrier and quickly recognizes the gray and white American Shorthair cat inside.

"What 'ya say we make a deal right here and now, dude?" Johnny raises his arms, encouraging. "Give me the eight bucks and, I'll hand over your kitty."

"That's my neighbor's cat." Paulo points at the pet carrier, deadpan serious.

The three boys look at each other, lost expressions with just a hint of panic now.

"Dude, he doesn't have a cat." Kevin expresses the bleak realization of their error. The cat meows again.

"You guys better take that cat back. Mrs. Johnson will be furious if she finds out you guys took Bootsy." Paulo, no longer entertained, warns sternly.

"Dude, he doesn't have a cat!" Kevin reiterates, sounding more anxious now.

"I told you guys this was a bad idea!" Louis finally voices his opinion. "We're all going to jail now thanks to you, Johnny, you ass!"

"Don't be such a whiny douche bag!" Johnny retorts, trying to keep his tough composure. "Nobody's going to jail, dude. We'll just take the cat back and let it go where we found it. We're just clowning dude, nobody's gonna hurt the cat."

"Hey guys," Paulo interrupts the teenage boys bickering, "let's get this straightened out. Tell you what." Paulo points at Johnny. "Isn't your mom an aerobics instructor?"

"Yeah." Johnny replies with a curious look.

"Okay," Paulo coolly poses, "She's into health and fitness stuff. So, here's what we're going to do. I will sell you a special order of my Herbalife vitamins and minerals package and include some very special, all organic perfume soap. The soap is very popular with the ladies right now. And I will include the soap for only half price. The value is worth many times more than the eight dollars I owe. I will sell a small container of vitamins, very cheap. We settle our differences this way, like businessmen."

The boys look at each other. Louis shrugs.

"My mom really likes that soap." Kevin nods, pushing his thick prescription glasses up against the bridge of his nose.

"Okay," Paulo points at Johnny again, "Johnny, you get an allowance, right?"

"Uh…" Johnny answers, "I work at the food court in Pleasant Hills Mall."

"Oh," Paulo charms, "a working man, cool. And you are going to be a Rockstar to your mom when you give the vitamins and soap to her."

"She actually does have a birthday coming up." Johnny nods, contemplating the matter and proposition at hand. "I do need to get on her good side. I want to borrow the car, now that I have my driver's license. I'm tired of always taking the bus."

"Yes, the bus sucks!" Paulo states. The boys chuckle in affirmation. Then, Paulo makes another proposition. "Let me have the cat and I will take him back to his home. We can meet at McDonald's on Jane Street by my house, this Saturday. You bring the money for the vitamins and soap. And your mom will be happy. Then, you will get to use your mom's car."

"I suppose that will make everything good." Johnny pouts, nodding in agreement.

"Of course, it will." Paulo replies, reaching for the carrier. "Who's pet carrier is this?"

"It's mine, I mean, my mom's." Kevin answers. "She has a cat. We borrowed it."

"Okay." Paulo takes the pet carrier in hand gently, trying not to disturb Bootsy. "Bring the money, twenty-seven dollars, and I will bring the pet carrier to McDonald's. So, your mom can get this back. Let's meet in the morning, ten o'clock, okay?"

The teenage boys all agree. They start to walk away, heading towards the bus stop.

"How did you guys know I was here, anyway?" Paulo asks, opening his car door.

"We left a note." Johnny replies. "We told you to meet us here."

"We put it on your front windshield." Kevin points at Paulo's car. Suddenly, Kevin's expression changes to a more, concerned look. "Uh…we, oh shit dude."

"Oh." Johnny responds, eyes wide, realizing another error has surfaced. "We thought that other, small white car was yours. It looks like yours."

"The white Volkswagen?" Paulo asks, having an idea what happened. "That's my other neighbor. Her car is different from my Nissan." Paulo points at his car.

"I guess they're both white and small." Kevin shrugs. "They all look alike. Our bad!"

"Okay, never mind." Paulo shakes his head. "I'll get it all straightened out."

Paulo cannot believe what has coincidentally transpired. Nevertheless, He knows what needs to be done. Paulo drives off, leaving the boys walking towards the bus stop. He hurries home and parks along the curve in front of his parents' house. Paulo walks to his neighbor's parked 2000 Volkswagen Beetle and retrieves the handwritten note the teenage boys placed. It was still clasped against the front windshield under the wiper blade, unnoticed by anyone. After breathing a sigh of relief, Paulo takes Bootsy out of the pet carrier and quietly places him down close to Mrs. Johnson's front porch. Paulo pets Bootsy and quietly apologizes for all the confusion and fuss. Bootsy meows and prances away, headed towards the side yard.

CHAPTER 8
HUSTLING ME FOR MONEY IS A NO-NO

Early Friday evening, October 5

Paulo is just leaving from his Herbalife meeting. He is thinking of Elvie. Paulo had called her late Wednesday night. He requested they all meet for dinner at the Marie Callender's in Ontario today. Realizing he is running late, Paulo hurries to his car and makes a quick call to let her know he is on his way to meet up with them. Elvie tells him they just arrived at the restaurant, and they will be there waiting for him. She tells Paulo to drive safely, not to rush.

Paulo is happy and very grateful to Elvie and Gigi. He knows that Elvie will listen to whatever is on his mind. She is genuinely full of good advice. Sometimes Paulo feels he can confide in her about his personal life more so than he can with his own father. Elvie is not judgmental, like his dad, Alejo. She doesn't criticize his shortcomings and mistakes in life. Elvie is encouraging, honestly offering what she feels is best for him, regarding his future goals and decisions. Sometimes though, she can be brutally honest.

Paulo is eager to meet the eldest sister of his mother for two reasons. First, Paulo wants extra cash. Although he has already paid Karen back for the upcoming concert tickets from his payday check, Paulo wants money to spend on his date with Karen on Sunday. Paulo is certain Elvie will enthusiastically support his amorous crusade.

The second reason he wants to meet up with Elvie is regarding a pressing matter he just can't get off his mind. Paulo wants to talk about the Almasi Ya Kifo diamonds. He misses having them in his possession more and more with each day that goes by. He's determined to have them back. Somehow, some way, he will find them. Paulo is certain his dear aunt can help. She initially recognized the rare gem's exclusivity. But she had encouraged and ultimately arranged for Paulo to get rid of them.

Paulo arrives at the restaurant where the hostess ushers him to Elvie and Gigi's table. The ladies smile brightly as soon as they see him.

Paulo greets them. "Hello Aunties, sorry for the wait. Nice to see you both again. Looking beautiful as always." He leans down to Elvie sitting in her stylish wheelchair and kisses her cheek. Then moves to Gigi and kisses her cheek.

"Oh, it's okay anak (*son*), they just sat us not too long ago. So, it's perfect." Elvie responds, adjusting her posture in the wheelchair. Gigi nods in agreement to what her partner has said.

Paulo takes his seat at the table and starts looking at the menu. He is hungry. The Marie's Meatloaf with mashed potatoes and fresh vegetables is looking good to him right now. After a few short minutes, they place their order with their waitress. They spend the time waiting for their dinner having amusing conversation, talking mostly about Paulo.

"So how are you Paulo? How is life at home with mom and dad? And your trip to Vegas?" Elvie inquires, anticipating a charismatic reply from him.

"Eh, I'm alright." Paulo sighs. "Life at home is okay. To be honest, I wish I had my own place. Hopefully, soon. And the Vegas trip was fun. Thanks to you and mom." He nods with a grin. But Paulo didn't share how he gambled all night and, barely had enough money to make it back home.

"Good to know. I'm sure you will get your own place when the right time comes." Elvie replies with a reassuring smile.

"Give it more time, Paulo." Gigi nods and smiles as well.

"I guess." Paulo acknowledges, appreciating their encouragement.

Elvie starts to talk about the good old days, when Paulo and his mother lived with her. She shares what a cute baby Paulo was and how he was such a good boy. She recalls how Paulo seldom cried, only when he was hungry or when it was time to change his diapers.

"It was a joy to watch you at a very young age, Paulo. I have lots of good memories." Elvie pleasantly recalls, taking firm hold of Paulo's hand. "Life was tough, but your mom and I had to maintain a good and positive attitude, and, in the end, everything worked out for us."

Their food is served. Everything smells as wonderful as it looks. Paulo has a satisfying smile on his face, as do Elvie and Gigi. They are all pleased to share this delightful meal together. Paulo politely takes this moment to thank them for meeting up with him for dinner.

They quietly begin to dine as Paulo turns the conversation more so, into a business matter. He asks the ladies if they both want to participate in the cruise ship game. He tells them the game has just started and this is the most advantageous opportunity to join. Nevertheless, they decline his fervent invitation. Elvie flat out refuses, saying she does not have time for such foolishness.

"Well then what about investing into my Amway or Herbalife? Sounds good, right? Yes?" Paulo nods with a zealous and insistent tone of voice.

"Paulo, I have enough business on my plate. I almost do not have time for myself." Elvie replies animatedly, while trying to keep her dinner napkin on her lap. Gigi notices it is about to slip away and fall to the floor. Gigi reaches over and delicately spreads the napkin across her partner's lap. The ladies clasp hands and smile at each other, chuckling.

"Ah, you're just like my mom, no time, no time." Paulo waves his hand in the same dismissive manner his father would have. "Okay. Just buy some vitamins or soaps, or lotions. Or all of the above. What do you think? I'll give you a discount." Paulo presses the matter.

Elvie and Gigi look at each other, astonished. They recognize that familiar tone of voice from Paulo when he needs money. Just like when he needed money to go to Las Vegas to meet up with Karen and her friends. No surprise, Paulo is hustling them again.

But this time, something seems different. Paulo is acting more insistent. "You are working and live at home." Elvie frowns, looking at Paulo. "What have you been doing with your money? Do your parents even know you have been meeting with me?"

Paulo says nothing. He takes a bite of some hot buttered cornbread. He manages only a slight shrug of his shoulders in response while he chews. Elvie is staring at him. She imagines the sweet little boy who used to live with her. She sees the darling godson she helped raise.

"Look, I don't want this to become your habit. I love and care about you. However, hustling me for money is a no-no." Elvie leans forward, looking directly at Paulo. "Whatever you need, I will lend you."

She asks how much he needs. Paulo answers, saying he needs two hundred dollars. Elvie agrees to give him the cash. Conditionally, she wants to be paid in full by the end of next month. Paulo agrees to her modest terms.

The waitress returns to their table and asks if any of them want dessert. They look at each other, smiling and giggling. The server smiles, presuming what their reply will be. Gigi and Paulo order from the restaurant's fresh baked pies menu. It will be a slice of Lemon Meringue pie for Gigi, her favorite. And for Paulo, a slice of the popular Chocolate Satin pie. Elvie orders a cup of black coffee. She has plans to sample at least a bite or two of Gigi's and Paulo's choices, of course.

After the waitress delivers dessert to their table Paulo starts talking about the mysterious diamonds. He concedes how much he thinks of them lately. He confesses how he wishes the diamonds were still in his possession. Then, he divulges something more profound. He is certain he can control and maintain his good luck next time, given another opportunity. Paulo asserts to Elvie quite frankly; she must get them back.

Elvie is perplexed. She doesn't know exactly what is happening to her nephew. But she recognizes one fact. Paulo has changed. More specifically, Paulo seems insistent to the point of being greedy right now. There is something else. Paulo's attitude has changed since he came into possession of the notorious Almasi Ya Kifo diamonds. There is no doubt about that.

Elvie is glaring at her nephew. Paulo can sense it, though he is not looking directly at her. But he knows; *if looks could kill, I'd be dead right now.* Nevertheless, her reaction does not dissuade him. Paulo continues telling Elvie that he can guarantee his diamonds will bring him great fortune. He avidly declares Elvie must have a positive attitude.

Elvie puts her right hand up to interrupt him. Paulo immediately stops talking. Gigi listens with a grin, quietly enjoying her creamy, sweet pie. The conversation is killed.

Elvie takes a slow, deep breath. *Help him to understand, instead of reprimanding him, like his father. He lacks wisdom.* She exhales the tension, fully.

"Listen Paulo, let me tell you a brief history about these diamonds you are talking about." Elvie gestures with pointed finger, continuing. "My grandmother used to have a respected fine jewelry shop in Angeles City, in the Philippines. Her shop was very famous with the wealthy aristocrats. And these diamonds were the talk of this community of rich women back then. The diamonds were known as the 'fate diamonds' and originated in South Africa. The woman who acquired them was the wife of a famous, but corrupt politician in my town. I heard from my grandmother that this politician spent a fortune to find these 'fate diamonds' just so his bratty wife could have them. They even hosted a big party so she could show off the diamonds. But a couple of days after the party, their house mysteriously burned down to the ground! Everybody perished, Paulo! During the investigation, as they searched through the ruins, they found the diamonds. It's the only thing they found that was still intact. And they looked untouched! Still shiny and beautiful in the burnt ruins!" Elvie affirms, eyes wide with a genuine hint of horror in reminiscence.

Paulo listens, keeping his attention primarily focused on his slice of delicious pie. He finally makes eye contact with Elvie when she is done talking and shrugs his shoulders.

"By the way, I don't know where the diamonds are now." She bluntly supplements.

Paulo nods slowly in acknowledgement.

They finish dessert with some pleasant small talk about Paulo's recent trip to Las Vegas, as a change of subject. Gigi takes care of the bill, and they prepare to leave. Paulo gets up and offers to wheel Elvie outside. They exit the restaurant together. Paulo pushes Elvie while Gigi walks alongside, towards their parked Cadillac SUV. Paulo kisses them goodbye. Elvie hands him two, crisp hundred-dollar bills and reminds him, it is a loan. Paulo graciously accepts the money, promising to repay her.

CHAPTER 9
THE ZEN OF XEN...

Next day, Saturday afternoon, October 6

PAULO IS PLAYING video games with Tommy at his apartment. They are enjoying some delivered pepperoni pizza, that Tommy had once again paid for. Next to the large box of pizza is an opened bag of potato chips, conveniently nestled between them to share as a side. They enjoy a couple cold canned beers, belching and laughing aloud as they talk trash about each other's video gaming skills. They're having fun.

They talk about going to the Bridge School concert in a few weeks with Karen. Tommy is also delighted to hear Paulo has a date with her tomorrow. He teases Paulo, things are getting serious it seems. Tommy can't help jesting his buddy just a little about how well things are going. He advises what his best friend's next move should be. Indeed, Tommy is always full of romantic advice, though he has been single for some time now. Nevertheless, he encourages Paulo to pursue a serious relationship with Karen. He knows Karen and Paulo will make a happy couple.

Their gaming session suddenly gets interrupted when Tommy's father walks into the room and asks his son for some help. Raymond had just stopped by to retrieve his computer that his son was working on. Tommy had upgraded his father's desktop hard drive. Raymond was ready to go back home however, he locked himself out of his pickup truck. But Raymond says the driver side window is cracked open just enough to maybe, get a hanger through the top. Tommy springs into action. He knows what to do. Tommy retrieves a wire hanger from the closet. His father takes a slice of pizza and a cold beer, as Tommy zips past him. Out the door like a blowing hooley, Tommy is on his way to save the day.

Paulo goes to the bathroom. He sits on the toilet and picks up one of the magazines from the small basket next to him. He notices someone that looks very familiar on the front cover. *Where did I see this woman?* Then, Paulo's eyes suddenly widen in stark recollection. *The transporter! This is the lady I bumped into!*

Pictured on the front cover of the magazine is fashion model Xenyatta Davenport. The same woman that he literally bumped into and inconspicuously stashed the Almasi Ya Kifo diamonds with at the Los Angeles International Airport.

"The Zen of Xen…" Paulo reads the front cover aloud and says, "she has my diamonds!"

Thoughts of retrieving the diamonds from the fashion model transporter fill Paulo's mind. He must talk to her. Paulo thinks of how he will demand to get his diamonds back when he sees her. He wants to tell her that he is the rightful owner of the Almasi Ya Kifo diamonds. Paulo really regrets following the adamant instructions of Elvie that day.

CHAPTER 10
THIS KID IS LOSING IT

Sunday morning, October 7

Elvie loves the weekend. She always enjoys spending time relaxing on beautiful days like today. Gigi is somewhat the opposite. She enjoys taking time to do her usual, weekend household chores. Gigi is getting things done, humming to the tunes of popular Filipino folk songs that are softly playing on the stereo CD player.

Elvie is content to sit in her quiet living room, enjoy her ice-cold Coke, and read. She was reading a couple new magazines that Gigi had placed on the coffee table for her. Three of the magazines, People, Newsweek, and Time, are the special 911 editions. After thumbing through those, Elvie decides to read something less troubling. She finds the perfect book to boost her mood. She retrieves a paperback book titled, *The Essays of a Chinese Woman Entrepreneur* from her Gucci bookbag next to the loveseat she is sitting on. With a smile, she opens the motivational read at the bookmark she had placed.

The author's story includes a collection of a dozen essays that are an inspiration to Elvie. The book is written by a successful Chinese businesswoman who has turned her hard-earned investments into a prosperous financial holding company. The author, Li Na Zhang holds several degrees, including a doctorate in business administration. Her book poses a narrative for Asian women entrepreneurs on how to collectively enable growth and success within their business practices. Elvie happened to meet Li Na Zhang at a professional leadership conference in Hong Kong, while traveling on business a few years ago. Elvie can directly relate to many of the author's experiences and challenges, expanding a wealthy business in Asia, within an industry that is predominantly male. Although Elvie's path to success in contrast was much more hostile than the path of the formally educated author she admires.

Suddenly, Elvie's cell phone rings, interrupting her quiet reflective moment. She is momentarily startled by the loud ringtone's intrusion. It's Paulo calling. Almost reluctantly, she answers the phone.

"Hey, do you know the transporter? Xenyatta Davenport. She is a famous model" Paulo abruptly greets. He is home watching WWE SmackDown on cable television.

"Excuse me, what did you just say?" Elvie retorts, frowning.

"Oh sorry. How are you today?" Paulo quickly changes his tone.

"That's better and I'm fine. Just relaxing." Elvie speaks up abruptly, "Oh, and I do not know the transporter personally, but I heard what happened in Italy. The person receiving the gem delivery freaked out when she saw the Almasi Ya Kifo diamonds. She refused them!"

Paulo is quiet. Nevertheless, he is not troubled hearing the disturbing update from her. Not the slightest. Paulo considers, perhaps the diamonds have returned to the United States with the model transporter, Xenyatta Davenport? His reaction is quite contrary to the privileged information he just heard. Paulo insists Elvie must find them now and get them back. He suggests they sell them and split the money. A reasonable plan.

Elvie's reaction is resolute.

"No Paulo. Even if I could, that is the last thing I would do. You understand?!" Elvie responds, raised voice.

Paulo hangs up.

"He hung up on me again!" Elvie looks at her phone. "Hmm…

this kid is losing it." She murmurs, putting her phone down on the coffee table. She calmly returns to reading her book.

CHAPTER 11
I HAVE TO GO!

Sunday evening, October 7 at the Red Onion in Santa Monica

It's 7:50 PM and California Calistoga has been playing an awesome set. The band covers popular alternative music from the 1990s to the enjoyable satisfaction of their audience this evening. Although the crowd isn't large, the indoor dining area allocated for the small concert is packed. The enlivening music fills the room like a pounding heartbeat. The crowd is energetic, nodding and swaying to the lively melodies. Everyone is drinking, dancing, laughing, and just having a great time.

Paulo and Karen have a small table to themselves near the entrance of the dining area. They continue much of their conversation from the enjoyable drive they had together. They are talking and laughing, finding humor in common, in just about anything that comes to mind. They are getting along, very well.

Paulo has had only one beer since they arrived for the start of the small concert. He drinks Diet Pepsi now but, he encourages Karen to have another beer. He wants to remain sober for their drive home. Karen surprises him completely with her response. She tells him he should relax and have another beer. Then she casually suggests they can always leave his car parked and, take a cab together in the morning to come and get it.

Paulo is slightly confused at first. Looking into Karen's eyes,

59

Paulo soon gets the message. There, in her eyes, Paulo finds a subtle, uncomplicated endorsement. Suddenly, he is charged with a sensation never felt before. Paulo has completely overcome the paralyzing nervousness he used to experience being around his boss at work.

The music tempo changes. The band plays a soothing cover of Baby, I Love Your Way by Peter Frampton. As the music begins, several couples walk towards a small section of the floor towards the front, that has been kept clear for dancing. Karen looks towards the front area at the band and smiles.

"I like this song." Karen takes hold of Paulo's hand. She stands and leads him to the small dance floor. Paulo goes, very willingly.

They embrace, finding themselves pressed closely together as a few more couples surround them on the floor. The music takes over. The flowing melody and lyrics are a mood, an aphrodisiac. Paulo cannot help but stare into Karen's eyes. She puts her arms around his neck as they sway together to the music. They stare. They smile. Their noses softly touch. Their lips meet. Paulo feels the delicious warmth of her tongue searching for his.

Paulo is holding her. His cheek is pressed against hers, snug. His arms pull her close again, as close and tight as she can physically be. They say nothing. There is no need for any more small talk this evening. The music plays, and they continue to sway, tenderly. In this delicate moment, they are falling for each other.

Paulo takes a glance at some of the people around him. He wonders if anyone here is as lucky and happy as he feels right now. He feels the warmth of Karen's body snug against his. He can feel her gentle breathing on his neck, she is so close. The sensation arouses the young man. *Damn the car keys! I'm ordering another beer!*

"I'm so glad we came here tonight, Paulo." Karen says, arms around his shoulders. "And thank you for driving. You know, you're really sweet. Especially at work, Paulo. You're such a gentleman." She smiles at him.

"I am?" Paulo is honestly surprised to hear that. If she only knew how dumbstruck and awkward he used to feel whenever she was around him.

They kiss again.

The song ends. Smiling, they release their tender embrace and walk hand in hand towards their table. Paulo pulls the seat for her to sit, very gentlemanlike. Karen sits and thanks him. She holds his hand as he takes his seat. They are looking into each other's eyes.

Karen is about to say something when she notices Paulo suddenly change his expression. He is looking past her shoulder in awe, eyes locked. He looks like he is about to gasp, wide eyed and slack jawed. Karen promptly turns to see what has captured Paulo's attention unexpectedly.

Strutting quickly towards them is a beautiful fashion model who has graced the front cover of many trendy magazines. She is Xenyatta Davenport. Karen recognizes her. Karen notices as she struts by, the model seems to be angry at something.

Xen is at the restaurant hosting a party for her boyfriend. Their party is going on in the adjacent, large VIP dining section. Xen and her boyfriend just had a falling out. And Xen has decided to leave her boyfriend there with his guests. Now she hurries past Paulo and Karen's table, headed towards the restaurant's main exit.

"I have to go!" It's all Paulo says. His eyes express something that has undoubtedly overcome him this very instant.

Karen doesn't know what is happening to Paulo. He seems frantic. She watches as he suddenly raises to his feet, almost toppling over the chair he was sitting in. Paulo turns to leave. He stops and looks back at Karen, about to speak. But he seems lost for words and says nothing. He turns to hurry away. He is engrossed in thought of something unseen.

"Paulo?" Karen calls out his name. She is about to ask him what is going on.

Paulo turns to look at Karen, waving his hand at her.

"Stay there, I'll be back."

Paulo turns back around and bumps into a server. The young man holding a tray with a couple empty glasses almost loses his balance. But he is somehow able to keep the glasses from falling off the tray onto the carpeted floor. Karen gasps at the sight of it all.

"Oh, sorry dude, my bad!" Paulo grabs and steadies the server.

Karen watches Paulo hurry through the exit doors. And he is suddenly gone.

Paulo hurries outside in time to see Xen as she gets into a small yellow cab. The door closes and the cab starts to move. It passes right in front of Paulo. He sees her, sitting in the back seat. Paulo perceives in that fleeting moment as the cab drives by, Xen seems to have something on her mind. *My diamonds!* He feels it.

Paulo runs to his parked car. First, he heads in the wrong direction. Then, remembering where he parked, he hurriedly saunters in the correct direction.

"My diamonds!" He says aloud, grabbing hold of his car door handle, "I know she has my diamonds! I need them back!"

Paulo starts his car and peels out of the parking lot. He turns in the direction he saw the cab last. Paulo finds it. There it is, not far in front, just down the busy street. With an eager smirk he steps on the gas pedal.

· · · · • · · ·

MEANWHILE, BACK AT the Red Onion, the band has finished their set. Karen sits at the small table, alone. She is quiet, thinking of what happened. Karen is certain that Paulo was staring at the beautiful cover girl. And it seems to Karen that Paulo went running after her.

Just then, the same server that Paulo almost knocked over comes to the table and asks her if she would like another drink. Karen shakes her head at first. Then she changes her mind and orders a Cosmopolitan. She looks at the large open doorway of the restaurant. *Where did he go?*

· · · · · **·** · · · ·

PAULO RACES THROUGH a red traffic light as the blaring horn sounds from another car that narrowly misses him. Paulo barely gives the loud swerving vehicle any attention. He stays focused on catching up to Xen's cab. He is intent on finding out where she is going right now. He must talk to her. Paulo will demand to have his diamonds back as soon as he can speak to her. He will tell her the gems were taken from him and transported without his consent. Paulo will tell her that he is the rightful owner of the Almasi Ya Kifo diamonds.

The yellow cab leads Paulo on a drive up to Lake Arrowhead. It's a beautiful night. The stars in the evening sky shine high above as they travel the windy mountain drive towards the lake resort area. Paulo is doing his best to stay close enough behind as not to get lost.

Suddenly, the yellow cab makes an abrupt turn that Paulo was not expecting. He tries to make an aggressive maneuver to follow. A car behind Paulo in the nearest lane veers to avoid a collision, its driver honking the horn in retort. During the evasive maneuver Paulo is distracted and, he has lost sight of the cab.

Paulo makes a sudden U-turn as soon as he is able. He races back to the street where the yellow cab turned. As soon as the traffic clears, Paulo screeches around the corner, heading down the street. He immediately notices a yellow cab, along with about half a dozen others that look exactly like the transporter's cab. He slows to a stop behind lots of traffic that he has just driven into. The street is very busy.

While he is stopped in bumper-to-bumper traffic, Paulo strains to see inside each of the cabs closest to him. He sees a woman seated in the back of one of them, a few car lengths ahead of his car. As the traffic slowly moves, Paulo gets his car into the same lane, right behind that cab. He smiles, relieved.

He continues to drive along with the slow-moving traffic, patiently waiting to see where the yellow cab he follows is going. Paulo is driving on the popular, scenic lakeside drive. It is a long road that winds around the large lake. The road he is on soon leads to the main intersection of the town. The road gets busy, packed with tourists every weekend when the weather is nice, like tonight.

The cab Paulo is following pulls to the curb in front of a restaurant and stops. He pulls up close to the cab and stops right behind it. The rear passenger door opens, and Paulo sees an attractive young lady step out of the vehicle. However, she is not Xen. The woman is quickly greeted by a few other people who are happy to see her. Paulo watches as they head into the restaurant. Next, the cab he was following drives off.

Paulo is feeling panicked. The transporter must be nearby. "Where is she?" He declares aloud as he puts his car into gear and pulls into the slow-moving traffic again. Paulo is looking left and right, searching desperately. He is looking into every cab, determined to find her again. "I know she's here somewhere!" He shouts out.

Paulo drives through the tourist town, passing through the busy, main intersection. He takes the scenic lake drive almost all the way round the lake. He thinks about going back the way he just came from, back into town. *Maybe she got out of her cab, and she is walking around town. I should go back.*

He decides to turn around. Paulo turns right at the next available corner. It is a lonely, dark road that leads to a small bridge. He immediately feels something. It is a familiar sensation. Paulo slows the car to a crawl. Down the darkened road, he barely sees some people standing close to the bridge he is approaching. His fingers begin to tingle.

· · · · **·** · · ·

Back at the Red Onion restaurant, Karen has been waiting for Paulo to return. She went outside to see if he was standing out there talking to the model. She noticed his car was gone. She walked back inside and sat at their table again in case he showed up.

After sitting a while, and a tall Cosmopolitan drink later, she decides to call his cell phone. Karen dials his number. Suddenly, she hears a mobile phone ringing. Karen turns around. There is no one. She turns about, looking for Paulo, perhaps standing nearby. The phone continues to ring over the crowded dining area noises. Karen listens carefully.

Looking out of curiosity under the table, she finds it. Paulo had dropped his cell phone. It's there, right next to his chair that he bumped into when he stood up to leave.

Karen finally decides to leave. She pays the check, tips the server, and walks out of the restaurant alone. Her date has abandoned her. The parking valet hails a cab for Karen. She looks at Paulo's cell phone as a yellow cab quickly pulls up to the curb next to her. She puts the phone into her purse. She sighs and gets into the vehicle. The cab drives away as she relaxes into the rear seat. Karen heads for home. It's going to be a long, lonely ride back.

CHAPTER 12
MY DIAMONDS

Paulo pulls over to the side of the road very slowly. He comes to a stop. He turns the headlights off, but the motor is still running. His car is far enough away from the people he sees that he will not be noticed. He quietly observes the people ahead of him. Then, he sees her.

"Oh!" Paulo utters aloud, leaning forward against the steering wheel. "There you are, pretty lady, I found you. This is fate! Yes!"

He smiles, anticipating he will be able to follow Xen again, and eventually talk to her. He will demand to know the whereabouts of his property, his treasured diamonds.

Paulo sees Xen walking with a man. He is her boyfriend. The couple are walking together on the same side of the road. They are crossing the bridge, walking away from Paulo's car.

There are three other people standing in the dark, on the other side of the road. Those people are standing on the same side of the bridge as Paulo's car.

One of those individuals Paulo sees is a man dressed in casual business suit. He happens to be the man that called Paulo, when Paulo still had the mysterious diamonds in his possession. Paulo had hung up on the man, thinking it was a menacing prank call arranged by Elvie. It was not a prank call.

The man Paulo sees standing in the dark is Chief Amitola. He is the brain trust within a tribal alliance to keep the mysterious Almasi Ya Kifo diamonds secretly hidden from main society. He is a key member of the Lake Arrowhead Paiute Tribe, entrusting the native peoples only use the diamonds in their rituals. The diamonds are only exposed during special occasions of celebration, then they are hidden away for the next occasion. They are not supposed to be taken away from the tribal chief's dwelling. In accordance with tradition, they are passed down through the generations.

There is a peculiar woman Paulo notices standing next to Chief Amitola. She is taller. She is dressed in a snug, long sleeve Habesha kemis style dress, with niqab style head dress, and gloves. She is covered from head to foot, entirely concealed. The mysterious woman is Shurze. She is Chief Amitola's confidant.

There is one more person there on a motorbike. He is stopped close to Chief Amitola and Shurze. That man is reformed convict, Mr. Angelino. He works for a covert delivery service.

Paulo carefully observes Chief Amitola place something into the motorcycle saddlebag. Then, Paulo hears the motorbike engine rev up, as it leaves the other two people there standing in the dark.

Paulo has arrived just in time to see a handoff. And it doesn't take much else to convince him so. He remembers the exchange in the terminal at Los Angeles International Airport. Sure thing, he instinctively knows what has just transpired.

He watches as the Harley-Davidson passes by him on the left. And as soon as it does, Paulo feels that bizarre sensation again. It's more intense this time. Liken to a summoning. His fingers begin to tingle again. He stares at the motorbike.

"My diamonds." He murmurs. Paulo turns his car around and follows the motorcycle.

· · · • · ·

NOT FAR AWAY, Mr. Angelino is stopping to get a quick bite. He turns his motorbike into the parking lot of an In-N-Out Burger joint. Paulo follows him, quickly turning close behind. Next, Mr. Angelino parks, dismounts his Harley, and casually walks inside the busy establishment. Paulo slowly backs into a nearby parking stall.

Paulo gets out of his car, leaving the engine running. He looks around to see if anyone is observing him. He glances at the restaurant door as he walks towards the Harley. Nobody is watching. He stands next to the motorcycle.

Paulo methodically reaches inside the saddlebag. He feels something. It's a velvet case. Paulo's heart starts to race with anticipation. Paulo feels the summoning intensify as he pulls the case out of the motorcycle saddlebag.

He immediately recognizes it. Paulo looks it over, smirking. His mouth is so dry, he can hardly swallow. His eyes widen, and his lips part with a whimper of selfish glee. Paulo feels complete satisfaction, just to hold them again.

Paulo doesn't waste time. He has retrieved the sole thing he has been looking for. He strolls to his parked car with haste. He glances around, trying not to be conspicuous. He gets into his car and firmly shuts the door. Again, he glances about him, sneering as if to warn others to stay away from him. Then he opens the black velvet case.

There before his eyes, are the Almasi Ya Kifo diamonds. The brilliant gems begin to sparkle, reflecting on his eyeballs, a radiance enchanting as a siren's chorus. Paulo is rapt.

"My diamonds." Paulo snickers. "I knew I would find you again!"

Paulo looks at the parked Harley. The motorbike driver is still inside the burger joint, nowhere to be seen. Paulo snaps the case closed. He puts his car into gear and quickly drives off.

ACKNOWLEDGMENTS

To our publishing consultant and editor, Barbara Lynn. Thank you for all your contributions and support during this creative process. You have once again made this a delightful experience. Our world is a better place because of you!

Do not be overcome by evil, but overcome evil with good.

Romans 12:21

New King James Version

THE FATE DIAMOND SERIES BOOK 1
ALMASI YA KIFO

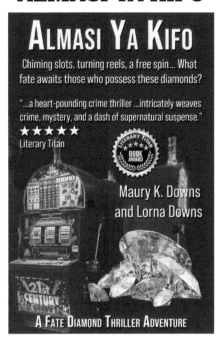

The Almasi Ya Kifo diamonds, respected, esteemed and celebrated by many... feared and cursed by others. Paulo Pineda is a popular and likable, but somewhat hesitant, young man incessantly seeking quick fortune. Joseph Ashe has more enemies than he has friends. He is not a popular, likable person, with a criminal record going way back. He recently came into possession of the mysterious Almasi Ya Kifo diamonds, having stolen them from his shady business partner. Quite unexpectantly, Paulo's and Joseph's paths collide, with dramatic affect. Now in possession of the diamonds, Paulo's life turns into a roller coaster adventure... both exhilarating and terrifying.

THE FATE DIAMOND SERIES BOOK 2

XENTASTIC

Xenyatta Davenport, (Xen to those that know her) is a well-known fashion model. She also has a covert side profession: transporting precious gems for insurance companies. Xen is in Italy to complete her latest secret assignment, however her Italian contact becomes fearfully alarmed to recognize the cursed Almasi Ya Kifo diamonds are part of the delivery. She vehemently refuses to accept the diamonds and thrusts them back to Xen. Xen had unknowingly received the mysterious Almasi Ya Kifo diamonds as part of her assignment. Now Xen is wondering how she ended up with them. Like others before her, Xen will experience some of the strange energy that the diamonds retain. What will those effects be… enchanting or precarious?

COMING SOON
THE FATE DIAMOND SERIES BOOK 4
MIRROR: A REFLECTION OF FATE

Once again, Paulo is in possession of the notorious Almasi Ya Kifo diamonds. He has incessantly wished for the bewitching stones to return to him practically from the moment he gave them up. Paulo is certain he can command providence and yield great fortune this time around.

Then he discovers something totally unexpected and remarkable. There seems to be an ulterior reason as to why he found the notorious fate diamonds again. Apparently, the stones have found their way back to the person that once happened upon them some years ago - his aunt Elvie.

After serious calamitous incidents occur in his personal life, Paulo is contacted by Chief Amitola of the Paiutes. He is given an ultimatum regarding his disposition and circumstances. What path will Paulo choose now? It is totally up to him. His fate is in his own hands.

ALSO BY MAURY K. DOWNS

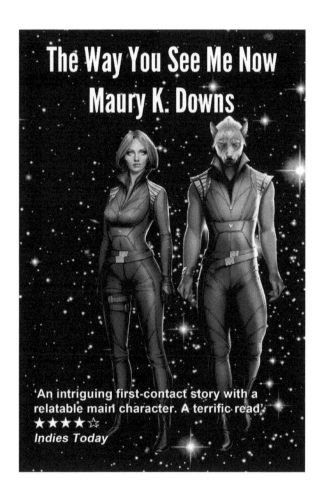

Aliens make a stealth landing late at night. They possess a unique capability never seen before. The mission becomes compromised when Brian discovers their presence. The aliens confront him, but he's unharmed. The aliens decide to continue with the mission and solicit Brian's help. Will they complete their important mission? Only destiny knows.

Milton Keynes UK
Ingram Content Group UK Ltd.
UKHW030904141024
449705UK00012B/575